TRAPPED IN THE OVERWORLD

TRAPPED IN THE OVERWORLD

AN UNOFFICIAL MINETRAPPED ADVENTURE, # 1

Winter Morgan

Sky Pony Press
New York

Copyright © 2016 by Hollan Publishing, Inc.

First box set edition 2017.

Minecraft® is a registered trademark of Notch Development AB.

The Minecraft game is copyright © Mojang AB.

Sky Pony Press books may be purchased in bulk at special discounts for sales promotion, corporate
gifts, fund-raising, or educational purposes. Special editions can also be created to specifications.
For details, contact the Special Sales Department, Sky Pony Press, 307 West 36th Street, 11th
Floor, New York, NY 10018 or info@skyhorsepublishing.com.

Sky Pony® is a registered trademark of Skyhorse Publishing, Inc.®, a Delaware corporation.

Minecraft® is a registered trademark of Notch Development AB.
The Minecraft game is copyright © Mojang AB.

Visit our website at www.skyponypress.com.

10 9 8 7 6 5 4 3 2 1

Library of Congress Cataloging-in-Publication Data

Names: Morgan, Winter, author.
Title: Trapped in the overworld / Winter Morgan.
Description: New York : Skyhorse Publishing, Inc., 2016. | Series: Unofficial
   minetrapped adventure series ; 1
Identifiers: LCCN 2015050171 (print) | LCCN 2016020855 (ebook) | ISBN
   9781510705975 (paperback) | ISBN 9781510706071 (ebook) | ISBN
   9781510706071
Subjects: | BISAC: JUVENILE FICTION / Action & Adventure / General. |
   JUVENILE FICTION / Action & Adventure / Survival Stories. | JUVENILE
   FICTION / Fantasy & Magic.
Classification: LCC PZ7.1.M6698 Tr 2016 (print) | LCC PZ7.1.M6698 (ebook) |
   DDC [Fic]--dc23
LC record available at https://lccn.loc.gov/2016010467

Cover design by Brian Peterson
Cover photo by Megan Miller

Box Set ISBN: 978-1-5107-2714-4

Printed in China

TABLE OF CONTENTS

TRAPPED IN THE OVERWORLD

1

AFTER SCHOOL

Simon had already gotten two warnings from his teacher about passing notes, but he couldn't help himself. He did want to learn about long division, but he also wanted to remind his friends Lily and Michael about the Minecraft game they had scheduled after school that day. Simon had spent the last few months playing with his friends on a multiplayer server where they had created a small town. Today they were going to finish a large roller coaster they were building outside of the village. Simon couldn't wait to test the roller coaster. He had to remind his friends about the meet up. When the teacher wasn't looking, he quickly tore a piece of paper from his notebook and ripped it in two. He wrote the same message on both sheets: "4pm. Today. Meet in the Overworld. Let's ride the coaster."

As Simon's teacher discussed a long-division problem on the blackboard, he passed the first note to Lily, who sat next to him. She read it and nodded her head. Simon knew passing the second note was going to be a bit more complicated because Michael sat at another table. He looked over at Michael, who was busy trying to figure out the math problem on a piece of paper and didn't see Simon staring at him. Simon aimed and threw the note at Michael, but the teacher turned around and spotted the flying paper.

"What was that?" His teacher, Mrs. Sanders, asked, walking over to where the note had fallen on the floor. She picked it up and looked at the note, then asked, "Who wrote this?"

Simon's heart was racing. He sat silently and didn't raise his hand.

"Okay, I'm going to ask one more time. Who wrote this note?"

Again, nobody raised their hands.

"I told you guys, I don't like note-passing. You have to pay attention to get the most out of your education." Mrs. Sanders lectured the class on the importance of long division.

Simon didn't want to admit that he wrote the note. He already had two warnings and he could feel Mrs. Sanders staring at him.

"The class is going to lose recess if someone doesn't admit to throwing this note," Mrs. Sanders announced.

Simon panicked. He knew he might get sent down to the principal's office if he admitted that he wrote the note. He didn't know what to do, so he did nothing.

"Nobody will admit to writing this note?" Mrs. Sanders held the paper up, walking around the classroom to show the kids the note. Her red nail-polished fingers clutched the small piece of paper.

"Everyone is losing recess. You get to spend the half-hour you usually get to spend playing in the schoolyard, sitting in this class working on five long-division math problems I'll write on the board."

The class let out a collective groan.

Melanie, who sat next to Lily, raised her hand, "I don't want to be a snitch, but I think I know who wrote it."

Mrs. Sanders said, "Melanie, I want the person who wrote it to admit they were passing notes." Mrs. Sanders looked at the note again. She knew it was about Minecraft.

Simon looked down at his black t-shirt with an image of a creeper on it. He could feel Mrs. Sanders staring at him. Simon didn't want Melanie outing him in front of the class or telling everyone that he was responsible for the class losing recess after school.

Simon raised his hand and admitted, "I wrote the note."

"Thank you for admitting that you wrote it." Mrs. Sanders looked at Simon, and then said to the class, "You will have recess. But Simon, you must stay behind. I need to talk to you."

Simon sighed. He could see Michael staring at him and whispering, "I'm sorry."

The class left for recess and Simon stayed in his seat. Mrs. Sanders called him over to her desk. "Simon, please come here."

Simon walked with his head down. He feared what Mrs. Sanders would say. He didn't want her to call his parents or send him to the principal.

"Simon, I know you love Minecraft and you're very excited to play the game with your friends after school, but you have to pay attention in class. Math is a vital skill. You might even need to use a bit of math in Minecraft."

Simon thought about the ways he used math in Minecraft. He did need it when he was building and creating servers. He nodded. He knew Mrs. Sanders was right.

"Do I have to go to the principal's office?" he asked.

"No, you can go outside and join the others at recess. I am not giving you another warning. I was impressed that you took responsibility and admitted you were wrong in front of the class. Although you made a bad decision in writing the note, it shows good character that you admitted your fault. But if this happens again, you will go to the principal's office."

Simon promised he would never pass another note in class, and left to join his friends in the schoolyard.

"Simon," Lily shouted across the schoolyard.

Michael and Lily rushed toward him. "What happened?" asked Michael.

"Nothing, really," he replied. "But that was pretty awful, wasn't it?"

"Yes," Lily agreed. "You can't pass notes anymore."

"If I had only caught it, everything would have been fine," Michael apologized.

"That's not the point," Lily remarked. "Simon shouldn't be passing notes at all."

"Agreed," Simon said. He quickly added, "I am so excited to ride the new coaster."

"Me, too." Michael was talking about the most recent updates he had made to the ride, when Melanie walked over to them.

"Didn't you learn the first two times you got in trouble? Passing notes isn't allowed in class," Melanie said matter-of-factly.

Simon had been avoiding Melanie since kindergarten, when she was labeled the class snitch. Now they were in fifth grade, and she was still telling on people. "You should mind your own business, Melanie."

Melanie just shrugged and walked away.

Just then, the lunchroom monitor announced that everyone had to go inside for lunch. The gang walked into the lunchroom and got in line.

"I hope they have chocolate milk today," said Lily.

"How can you think about chocolate milk when we're going to test out the most extreme roller coaster in Minecraft? Man, everyone on our server is going to be jealous of us." Simon rattled on about the ride.

"I hope nobody destroyed it. You know how much I hate griefers," Lily remarked.

Simon's jaw dropped. It had never occurred to him that a griefer might destroy his coaster, but now it was all he could think about. He couldn't concentrate for the rest of the school day. He was too preoccupied with his roller coaster. He couldn't wait to get home and see if it was still functioning.

2
LIGHTNING STRIKES

When the school day finally ended, Simon rushed home and turned on his computer. Lily and Michael weren't on the server yet. In the Minecraft world, his name was HeroSi, Lily was QueenLil, and Michael was DiamondHunter. The group always stuck together and went on numerous treasure hunts.

HeroSi had a large house and a farm where he grew potatoes and carrots. He also had a flock of sheep and an ocelot named Meow. Simon loved his Minecraft world. It was his escape from the real world, where Mrs. Sanders forced him to learn long division, and where his parents reminded him to do his chores. In fact, he knew he needed to take out the recycling right after he finished his Minecraft game. He was only allowed to play for one hour and then his screen time was over.

Simon was relieved to find the coaster still intact—nobody had destroyed it. With a smile, he began to add the finishing touches to the ride.

A message popped on the screen. His friends were on the server.

"Are you excited to test out the coaster?" asked Simon.

"Is it done?" Michael replied.

"Almost." Simon finished the last of the minecarts they would ride in. "Now it's done."

Simon, Lily, and Michael hopped into one minecart, cheering, "Let's go!"

The trio rode in the coaster. Simon let out a scream as his and his friends' characters went down the first big drop on screen, and he was glad his friends couldn't hear him.

The roller coaster climbed toward its second big drop and Simon couldn't wait until they reached the top.

"We're almost there," said Lily.

"I know! This rocks," added Michael.

"Whee!" Simon was thrilled as they reached the bottom of the biggest drop.

The ride was over. Simon could barely believe that they hadn't ridden an actual roller coaster. Although it was crafted on the computer, he had felt all the drops.

"Now that we've ridden it, we have to come up with a name. What should we name the coaster?" Lily loved naming everything. She had named their town, their houses, and all the pets. She had even named Simon's ocelot "Meow."

"The Big Dipper?" suggested Michael.

"I think that one's been used. Let's make up something really cool." Lily said and then followed it with a list of potential names, "The Flyer, Dropper—"

"Let's not worry about names right now," Michael said. "I just want to ride it again!"

"Okay," Lily replied, and they all hopped in the minecart for another ride on the unnamed coaster.

Simon thought the coaster was better the second time around because he didn't have to worry if there were any glitches, and he knew he was in for a smooth ride.

"Again?" asked Simon. But before he could hop into the minecart for a third ride, his mother walked into their small home office, where they kept the family computer.

"Simon, you have to get off the computer. There's been a tornado warning."

"A tornado?" Simon couldn't believe it. There were never severe storms in his part of the country. "Are you sure?"

"Yes, the news is warning everyone. We have to get to a safe spot in the house. Your brother is already in the basement. Come quickly." Her voice shook, and she sounded very nervous.

"Guys, did you hear there is a tornado warning?" Simon asked Michael and Lily.

"What? How do you know?" Michael hadn't heard about the warning.

"My mom just told me. I have to shut off the computer and go to the basement."

"My dad just told me that we have to go to the basement, too," Lily said, just as they all heard the crash of thunder in the distance.

"Wait. Do you see that person near the coaster?" Michael asked them.

Simon looked at his computer screen. There was a person dressed in a green jumpsuit walking toward the coaster. He was carrying what looked like a brick of TNT.

"We can't leave. That looks like a griefer," Lily remarked. "But my dad is really upset. He says we have to get to the basement as fast as we can because the storm is approaching."

Simon could hear his mother shout his name from the basement. "Where are you? This isn't a joke! You could get seriously hurt."

Simon knew his mom was right, but there was someone about to blow their coaster up. They had worked on that roller coaster for three months. He didn't know what to do.

"Michael, Lily. Are you still there?" he asked.

"Yes," they both replied.

"We have to stop this griefer now." Simon grabbed his diamond sword and dashed toward the person in the green jumpsuit.

Michael and Lily joined their friend. As the trio leapt at the griefer, he grabbed a bottle from his inventory and splashed a potion of weakness on the gang.

They grew frail, but they still had enough energy to strike the griefer with their diamond swords.

"He's not alone," Michael spotted another person in a green jumpsuit carrying bricks of TNT.

Lily used her last bit of energy to move toward the other griefer. She lunged at him, destroying the griefer with her diamond sword.

"Good job," Simon told Lily as she ran back to help her friends battle the stronger griefer.

"Simon!" His mother hollered from the basement, "Get down here!"

The sound of thunder boomed through the house again. "Did you hear that, guys?" Simon asked his friends.

"It sounds like a TNT explosion, but it's coming from the real world," Lily wrote. "My dad is calling me."

"I got him." Michael was lost in the game, not paying attention to the storm. He struck the griefer and destroyed him.

"Simon!" His mother sounded frantic, her voice halfway drowned out by another peal of thunder. The lights and the computer screen flickered as lightning lit up the sky.

Simon was starting to shut the game down, already reaching for the computer's power button, when a lightning bolt struck the house and the lights went out completely. He fell to the ground. That was the last thing he remembered.

3
STRANGE STORMS

"Simon!"

Simon thought his mother was calling his name, but when he opened his eyes, he saw Lily.

"Lily, what are you doing here?" Simon was confused.

Michael stood next to Lily at the foot of a large roller coaster. Though Simon remembered a thunderstorm, the sky over their heads was sunny and dotted with clouds. "Do you realize what's happened to us?"

"No," Simon looked around. "Where are we?"

Lily shook her head in disbelief. "I think we're *in* Minecraft."

"What?" Simon looked around. He wasn't sure what had happened to them.

"We're in Lisimi Village," Lily announced.

Lily had named their town Lisimi Village after the group of friends, taking the first two letters from each of their names and putting them together to create the name.

"How did we wind up inside a game? That seems impossible." Simon walked around the coaster. He couldn't believe he was actually in Lisimi Village, standing next to the ride he had crafted.

"Maybe it was the storm?" Michael theorized. "Did you ever make it to the basement?"

"No, the last thing I remember was my mom calling my name and a lightning bolt striking our house and shutting off our electricity. We had a blackout. My mom and brother were in the basement with the flashlights, but I never made it down there."

"Do you think we're trapped here?" Lily's voice trembled.

"I don't know, but I want to go home. My mom must be really upset." Simon paced as he spoke.

"My dad is probably worried sick about where I am. He'd never think to look in my Minecraft game," Lily said.

"Don't worry," Michael reassured Lily. "Everything is going to be okay. We'll get out of here."

"But how? There's no way out!" Lily replied.

Michael paused, "Don't say that. We could . . ." But he had no ideas.

"I'm sure we'll find a way to leave the game. Let's brainstorm," Simon suggested.

"Maybe there will be another lightning bolt and we'll fall out of the game, just like we fell in," Lily said.

"I don't think we can count on that," Simon stifled back tears. "We have to come up with a more strategic plan."

Michael looked at the coaster. "Since we're here, maybe we should ride the coaster? I mean, it stinks that we're trapped here, but we should try to have some fun."

Lily squared her shoulders and nodded. "Yes, that does sound like fun."

Simon wiped a tear from his eyes. He wanted to keep looking for a way out, but when his friends hopped into the minecarts, he reluctantly joined them to ride the coaster. Simon had to admit, this was like a dream come true. Despite the nightmare of being trapped in the Overworld, he was excited to ride in a minecart without having to sit at his computer and navigate into it.

But as they made their first big drop, Lily called out, "Oh no!"

"What? It's not that scary," said Michael.

"No! I see the griefer in the green jumpsuit." Her voice shook. "What will happen to us if he destroys the coaster, and we're on it?"

They soared down the second drop. Simon could feel his stomach clenching in fear, and he wanted to stop the coaster, but it was slowly creeping up toward the final drop. Simon knew he had to wait for the ride to be over. If they jumped out of the minecart, they'd be destroyed, and he wasn't sure where they would respawn.

Simon had an idea. "Guys, if we get destroyed, do you think we'll respawn in our beds at home?"

"I'm not sure, but we're probably going to find out," Lily answered.

As the coaster dropped, Simon could see the griefer placing the brick of TNT at the bottom of the incline. "We have to be ready to jump off the ride," he said.

Simon waited for just the right moment, when the coaster had dropped low enough for them to jump off without getting hurt, and yelled, "Jump off!"

Lily, Michael, and Simon leapt from the coaster and landed next to the griefer in the green jumpsuit.

Simon took out his diamond sword. "You're not blowing up our ride."

The griefer fled. Simon raced after him as Michael grabbed the TNT the griefer left behind and placed it in his inventory.

"We have to stop him!" Simon said breathlessly as he chased the griefer away from the village. The sword felt heavier than he had imagined when he was play-ing the game. He was tired as he sprinted through the biome, and his enchanted diamond sword slowed him down.

Simon felt odd running in the Overworld. His feet didn't feel like his feet did in the real world. The blocky ground seemed harder, even though he was running through the grassy biome. Everything felt different.

Simon didn't like this new feeling, and he didn't want to get used to it; he wanted to go home. But for the moment, he had no choice. He had to battle this griefer before he could figure out a plan of escape.

As Simon began to catch up, the griefer stopped and splashed a potion of weakness at Simon. He couldn't move.

"Help!" Simon called out.

His friends raced to his side. Michael gave him some milk, and Lily aimed her bow and arrow at the griefer. She struck him with her arrow, destroying the man in the green jumpsuit.

"Now that the griefer is gone, we have to figure out how to get out of here."

"Ow!" Lily grabbed her arm. "I was just struck by an arrow."

A horde of people in green jumpsuits ran toward them. As arrows shot at Simon, he tried to drink enough milk to keep up his strength, but he was losing hearts.

Michael called out, "We need a potion of invisibility."

Lily replied, "I don't have one."

"Me, neither," added Michael.

Lily rushed toward the griefers, but she was no match for the army that was attacking them.

The army flung a sea of arrows at Simon. He couldn't fight back.

"Simon!" Michael yelled. "Dodge the arrows!"

"I can't! I'm about to be destroyed," Simon said— and then he faded away.

4
FAMILIAR LANDSCAPE

Simon respawned. Before he opened his eyes, he knew where he was, and it made him very upset. He was hoping he would wake up in his bed, with his cool blue sheets covered in stars and constellations, but that wasn't the case. Simon was covered in a red wool blanket—a blanket from his house in the Overworld.

He remembered the months he had spent constructing this house. He had used up his entire screen-time limit placing emeralds on the walls and building furniture. The large picture window he had made looked out at his friends' homes. And though Simon wanted his friends to respawn in their beds in the real world, he knew they'd probably land in their Minecraft homes, too.

Grimly, Simon opened his eyes and walked out of his house to look for Lily and Michael.

He sighed and said, to nobody in particular, "I used to dream about actually walking around my Minecraft house, and now I just want to leave Lisimi Village."

Simon walked toward his friends' homes, but paused when he felt an arrow pierce his arm. "Ouch!" He rubbed the place where the arrow had struck him.

"Watch out!" Lily hollered as she scampered out of her home. "The griefers are back."

Michael opened the door of his epic wooden home and joined his friends. He grabbed his diamond sword and said, "We have to destroy them."

"We have to get back to the real world," Simon said as he raced alongside Michael and Lily.

"That's true," Lily ran toward the griefers. "But first we have to battle these guys."

"Who knows? Maybe they are responsible for us being here," Michael called out as he held his diamond sword and raced toward their enemy.

"Do you really think so?" Simon asked. The thought infuriated him. He wanted to punish these griefers for trapping them in the Overworld.

Simon struck one of the griefers with his enchanted diamond sword. It hit the arm of the griefer, who shouted, "You can't just show up and expect to overthrow us! We've been here for a very long time."

"Are you stuck here, too?" asked Simon.

At that, the green griefer looked surprised, and put his sword down. He called to the others to stop fighting. "Everyone, these aren't our enemies. We must stop battling them."

Lily and Michael were confused that the skirmish was over, when it hadn't even really begun.

The griefer who had put his sword down said, "These are other people trapped in the game."

The group of green-suited people let out a collective sound of shock. Some of them gasped; others insisted that Simon wasn't telling the truth.

Simon said, "We are trapped in the Overworld. Normally, this would have been a dream for us. All three of us are obsessed with playing Minecraft, but now we are really sad. We miss our families and we know they are probably very worried about us. Even worse, we have no idea if the people we left behind are even safe, because when we were transported to the Overworld, there was a horrible storm in our neighborhood."

"It was a tornado," Lily added. "And there was a lot of lightning."

Michael said, "We kept playing on our server when we should have been in our basements, sheltering ourselves from the storm."

Simon realized that, in a way, these green griefers actually were responsible for them being trapped in the Overworld. If they hadn't been trying to blow up the roller coaster, Simon and his friends wouldn't have stayed on the server. Simon explained this to the griefers.

One of the griefers replied, "We didn't know you were in the middle of a storm. You could have stopped playing."

Simon was annoyed. He wanted the griefers to take responsibility for his friends being trapped in the Minecraft game, but he had to admit that it was also their own fault. It was just a game, and they could have walked away. Although it took them ages to construct the roller coaster, they probably shouldn't have built something so valuable on a public server in Survival mode. It was pointless to spend the day placing blame, when both the griefers and Simon's friends were at fault.

Lily seemed to have reached the same conclusion. She raised her voice. "Stop it! It doesn't matter who is responsible for us being here. We just have to focus on getting back home."

"You know a way for us to get back home?" one of the griefers asked hopefully.

Michael asked, "Do you mean that you don't?"

A griefer replied, "No, we are all trapped. It's awful. We have been here for a very long time. In fact, we've lost track of time."

"That's awful," Lily said.

"We gave up trying to get back home a long time ago," said another griefer.

"How were you trapped to begin with?" Lily couldn't believe all of these players had been sucked into the Overworld like she and her friends had.

Everyone had the same story. They had been zapped into the game during a storm.

Michael asked, "How did you meet?"

"We were all imprisoned by a very mean person who controls this server. We don't even know who he is, because he never told us his name. He found us all when we were first trapped here. He's the most evil griefer I've ever encountered." The griefer shuddered when he spoke about the man who had locked them up.

Another griefer said, "When we were trapped, we began to plot our escape. We decided to change our skins to match each other."

A female griefer from the group called out, "Once we did that, we named ourselves the Prismarines."

"Do you each have names?" asked Michael

"Yes, I'm Brett," said the first griefer they had talked to. He continued, "When we changed our skins to match each other, we were also planning to escape from the evil griefer's prison."

"Where was the prison?" questioned Simon.

"It was in the middle of the jungle. The mean griefer has an enormous jungle temple. You've never seen anything as large as this temple. He added on to one that had been built. He placed us in a cell in the basement." Brett spoke quickly, explaining how they had been locked up and given very little food.

"It was the worst," another Prismarine confirmed. "But we realized that if we all looked alike, we could attack the mean griefer and he'd never know which of us did it."

"That sounds like a good plan," Simon said. "But what are you doing to destroy him, and how do you plan on getting back to the real world?"

They all started to talk at once.

Lily yelled, "Stop. We have no idea what you're saying."

They were too busy talking to notice Lily's comment. Only when they heard a loud explosion did the Prismarines fall silent.

Kaboom!

The sound pierced their ears, and they looked around to see what had been blown up.

Simon cried out, "My house!"

5
BURNING DOWN THE HOUSE

Simon dashed toward his house. He inspected the rubble and shouted to the Prismarines who crowded around him, "You were distracting us. You wanted this to happen. You just love blowing things up!"

"No, we don't," said Brett.

"That's a lie. You tried blowing up our roller coaster." Simon stood next to the remnants of his house. Not only was he trapped in the Overworld, now he didn't even have the comfort of staying in the house he had spent months constructing. And he had lost all of the emeralds that adorned his walls. He had planned to remove the emeralds and trade them for valuable resources in the village, but now he couldn't. He was devastated.

The Prismarines tried to defend themselves. "It wasn't us. It's true that we tried to blow up your coaster, but that was because we were jealous that you weren't trapped in the Overworld, like we are. Now that we know you're one of us, we don't want to attack you. We want to work with you to get out of the Overworld and get back home," said Brett.

"We also need your help in battling the master-mind griefer. He's probably the one who is responsible for destroying your house," another Prismarine, who introduced herself as Greta, explained.

Simon's head was spinning. He didn't know whom to believe, or whom to trust. He only knew the facts. His house was destroyed, and the people in green jumpsuits that stood around him had attacked him once before. He didn't know what to do.

Then Greta suggested, "We can help you rebuild."

Simon hesitated, looking at the rubble that was once his beloved home. Then he sighed and replied, "Okay. Thanks."

"Can you lead us to the jungle temple where the master griefer kept you?" asked Lily.

One of the Prismarines started to shake when he replied, "Why? I don't want to go back there."

"But we have to stop him before he destroys any more of our property," said Lily.

"And I wonder if he's responsible for us being trapped on this server in the Overworld," Michael added. "If he was able to spot all of us when we were first sucked into the game, he might have a lot more control over the Minecraft world than we could imagine."

This comment stunned everyone. Michael stood before a sea of gaping mouths. Simon asked, "Do you think if we find him, we can actually make our way back to the real world?'

Michael replied, "I don't know, but we have to find out."

Before the group could come up with a plan to find the master griefer and force him to get them back to the real world, they heard a loud noise in the distance.

"Is that another explosion?" Lily looked up in shock.

"No," a Prismarine replied. "It sounds like thunder."

The sky grew dark and rain began to pound down on the group. They sprinted to Lily's house to get to shelter.

Everyone crowded into Lily's tiny living room. Lily had crafted a small cottage instead of a large house like Michael and Simon had each built. Lily's cottage had only two bedrooms, and was designed to look like the homes she rented with her parents and her sister by the beach every summer.

As the rain fell on the roof of the cottage, Lily remembered all of the summers she had spent at the beach with her family. They were the best times of her life, and she waited all school year to swim in the ocean and eat fresh fish. She had been looking forward to another vacation to the cottage this summer, but with escape from the Overworld looking unlikely, the beach now seemed like a distant part of her past.

Lily had to adjust to her new life in the Overworld or she wouldn't survive. If she kept thinking about the cottage at the beach, she'd be too sad to fight. And she had to fight, because she had to win. She couldn't let this master griefer get away with destroying everything they had in the Overworld, or keep her from getting home.

"Lily, I wish you'd built a bigger house," Simon complained. Something—maybe the wind—made the walls creak as he spoke.

"I'm sorry. I'm not like you and Michael. I don't need massive, epic homes that people talk about all over the Overworld. I like to live a modest life," Lily defended herself. She thought she saw movement in the darkness outside her window, and turned to look.

At that moment, a zombie ripped the front door from its hinges. Lily and her friends cried out in shock.

Simon leapt toward the zombie with his diamond sword. He struck the vacant-eyed undead mob and destroyed it. He looked outside and saw that Lisimi Village was teeming with skeletons and zombies. "We have to go out and battle. This rain has spawned a bunch of hostile mobs, and they are terrorizing the village."

Simon wondered if the master griefer was behind this attack. Could he have spawned these creatures? But Simon couldn't sit around and wonder why the monsters were in their village; he had to battle them.

The gang put on their armor and ran into the thick of the invasion. Lily struck a skeleton with her sword, but though it lost hearts, it wasn't destroyed. Another skeleton shot an arrow at her, and Lily's energy was fading. Simon joined her and helped defeat the bony beasts.

Michael called to his friends, "Help me. We have to save the town. The zombies are attacking the villagers and transforming them into zombies. Does everyone have golden apples?"

"I do," exclaimed Lily.

"Me too," said Simon.

Simon wanted to help the townspeople stay safe. He was friends with some of the villagers in Lisimi Village and didn't want to see them hurt. As the population of the town he, Lily, and Michael had built had grown, the group had become good friends with villagers like Fred the Farmer, who Simon spotted trying to escape from a zombie. He could see the brown-robed farmer fighting for his life.

"Fred!" Simon called out. "We're here to help!"

The trio raced toward the zombie that was attacking Fred and struck the large undead mob with their diamond swords, destroying it.

"Thank you," Fred said.

"Don't thank us," Simon responded. "Just get to shelter, quickly. We don't want you getting hurt."

Next door to Fred there lived a fisherwoman named Emily. Prepared for the worst, the group raced to Emily's house to see if she was okay.

As the group reached Emily's doorstep, the rain stopped and the hostile mobs disappeared. Emily's door was ajar, her house unusually dark inside.

"Emily?" Simon called to his friend as he pushed her door open, but there was no response. He walked inside, and the friends could hear him moving through the house's different rooms.

"Is she okay?" Fred called to Simon.

"She's not here," Simon said, emerging from Emily's house.

6
IT GETS REAL

"**W**here is Emily?" Fred was worried.

The Prismarines joined them, and Greta suggested, "It looks like the rain has stopped. We should head to the jungle to find the master griefer."

"We can't leave," Simon told them. "Our friend Emily is missing."

Michael said, "She was the best fisherwoman. She would catch so many fish and we'd cook these incredibly large dinners to share with all the townspeople and villagers. Those feasts are some of my favorite memories from the world of Minecraft—not at all like today."

Brett said, "We can't wait around to find your friend. We have to stop the master griefer. Now that you guys are here, he seems to be increasing his attacks."

"Really?" asked Lily.

"Yes. He trapped us and would stage battles, but he never blew up our homes or spawned hostile mobs," Greta explained.

Simon was conflicted. He didn't want to abandon his friend, Emily, who was missing and could have turned into a zombie villager. But he also wanted to go to the jungle biome to stop these attacks so he could figure out a way to go home.

"Just give us a short time to find Emily, and then we can head to the jungle biome with you," Simon pleaded.

The Prismarines talked among themselves and then one of them replied, "Okay, we'll help you find Emily. Then we'll all trek to the master griefer's lair. It's useless if we travel there on our own."

Simon walked through the village, calling Emily's name. All around him, the houses and shops of the town were damaged from the attack. Many buildings had their doors ripped off, and folks were busy repairing the damage. Simon saw his friend Juan the Butcher.

"Juan," Simon asked. "Have you seen Emily?"

"Yes," Juan replied. "I saw her early this morning, when she left to go on a fishing trip."

Simon was relieved to learn that Emily hadn't even been in the village during the attack. With a sigh of relief, he explained, "Juan. I'm not just a player anymore. I am actually living in Minecraft."

Juan gasped. "Not you, too!"

"You mean you've heard about people being trapped in the game before?" Simon couldn't believe it—he wanted to hear the entire story.

"Years ago, I heard there was a group of players that were pulled into the game."

"Did they get out?"

"Yes," Juan replied. "I heard they did."

"How?" Simon asked. He called the others over to hear the conversation.

"I think there is a very powerful, mean man that can zap you into the game, but he can also get you out," Juan told them.

"It must be the master griefer," one of the Prismarines called out.

"Does he have a name?" Simon asked.

"I believe his name is Mr. Anarchy," Juan said.

"I've never heard that name," Brett said.

"How did those people escape from the Overworld?" Simon didn't want to get distracted. He had one question that he wanted answered.

"I'm not sure. I think it had something to do with Mr. Anarchy. But it made him very angry. He staged many attacks on the Overworld. Ender Dragons and Withers flew through the skies of our village for years. Players never wanted to be on this server. I had no customers at my blacksmith shop."

"Do you know the people who escaped?" asked Lily.

"No, and I don't even know their names. I wish I did and I wish I could help you guys, but I've told you all that I know. I'm just a simple villager." Juan frowned. He really wanted to help them get back to the real world, but he also feared that Lisimi Village would suffer through endless attacks like it had in the past. Mr.

Anarchy was a serious menace to the Overworld, and because Juan was a villager, he had no home to escape to if Mr. Anarchy made the Overworld unlivable.

"You've been a huge help already," Simon told Juan. To the group, he said, "I think we know what we need to do now. Now that we know Emily is safe, we must head to the jungle."

Brett studied a map to the jungle temple. "I really don't think I can go back there."

Simon paused, and then suggested, "That's okay. If you give us the map, your group could stay here and protect the town. My friends, Lily and Michael, and I will head to the jungle on our own. We want to surprise Mr. Anarchy. Once we get there, we will find him, and when we start to battle, we'll ask you to TP to the jungle to join us."

Brett was relieved, but the rest of the Prismarines weren't too pleased with this idea. They wanted to travel to the jungle, too, but they realized Simon was right. If they all traveled together, Mr. Anarchy might be suspicious. Before they met this trio, they hadn't even known the master griefer's name. They felt like these new friends might be bringing them closer to getting back home.

Greta asked if they had enough supplies. Simon, Michael, and Lily looked through their inventories and realized they were missing potions and were running low on food.

As the folks in green jumpsuits restocked their inventories, the gang was thankful that these old enemies had become new friends.

7
IGLOO

"**E**mily!" Simon spotted his friend at the shore as they made their way towards the jungle biome. She was about to cast and, from the looks of the pile by her side, she had already caught an abundance of fish.

"Simon, Lily, and Michael!" Emily put down her fishing rod. "How are you?"

Lily replied, "We're not so good. We're trapped in the Overworld and we want to get home desperately."

"That sounds like the work of Mr. Anarchy," Emily said. "Have you heard of him?"

"Yes, Juan told us all about him," Simon told his fisherwoman friend.

"Well, he's a very powerful man. I used to be friends with him," said Emily.

"You did?" Lily was shocked.

"Yes. Years ago, when he was a player, he would trade his emeralds for fish."

"Why did he become so evil?" questioned Michael.

"That's a good question. He became evil because he realized that he'd be trapped in the game forever. When he tried to leave the game, he was only able to let others out and bring others in, but he couldn't leave. At first he loved his power, but when he realized he could never go home again, he turned into a very bad man."

"I feel bad for him," Lily said. "Maybe we can help him."

"Feel bad for him? He is probably the person responsible for zapping us into this game and trapping us here." Michael was annoyed.

"And he blew up my house!" Simon added angrily.

"He also caused a lot of damage in the Overworld, which our friends are trying to repair right now. And who knows what he is going to do next? And you feel bad for him?" Michael was perplexed.

"We've only been here a very short while. Maybe if we knew we were trapped here forever, we might turn into evil people," Lily explained.

"But it's how someone reacts when something bad happens that shows their true character," said Simon.

"Yes, Mr. Anarchy has very bad character," added Michael. "I think none of us would turn into evil people if we found out we were trapped here forever." Michael truly believed this. Although he feared being trapped in this world forever, he knew that it wouldn't change him into a horrible person. He never contemplated becoming a griefer, and he always wanted to help others.

"You say that now," Lily responded, "but you don't really know. At this point, we all have hope. Once that hope runs out, we might turn into different people."

"Hope will never run out. I believe we'll get out of here," Michael said. He turned to Emily. "We have to go to the jungle. It was nice seeing you."

Emily offered the trio some fish she had caught. "Place these in your inventory. You need to have something for dinner. Also, find a place to build a house. It's almost nighttime, and you don't want to leave yourselves vulnerable to hostile mob invasions."

They thanked Emily. Lily studied the map. "It looks like there is a cold biome over this mountain. Let's build a house over there."

"I've always wanted to build an igloo," Michael said enthusiastically.

The group trekked toward the cold biome and over the steep mountain. Simon paused at the top of the mountain. "The Overworld is so massive."

Lily looked at the map. "And we have a long journey before we reach the jungle biome. We don't have time to stop and stare at the scenery."

"You're right. We don't want to be out at night, when witches spawn." Simon carefully climbed down the mountain.

"I definitely don't," Lily said. "Remember how terrified I am of witches when we play this game together?

I can't imagine what it would be like to actually face one in real life." She shuddered.

"Hopefully, we'll never have to find out," Simon said.

"This looks like a great spot to build our igloo," suggested Michael. He started pulling the necessary supplies from his inventory, while Lily and Simon gathered blocks of snow.

Suddenly, they heard a noise in the distance. It sounded like a howl.

The skin on the three friends' necks prickled, and they stopped what they were doing to look out into the darkening cold biome.

Suddenly, an animal raced by them.

"Did you see that?" asked Lily.

There was a growl, and the animal ran past again. Its coat was gray, and it was quite muscular. It made its way through the snow swiftly.

"I think it's a wolf," Simon said.

"Let's tame it!" Instead of being scared, Lily was excited to tame the wolf. She had never tamed an animal before. Simon had his pet ocelot, which he had tamed and Lily always played with, but she didn't have a pet of her own.

Lily grabbed bones from her inventory and leaned down in the snow, offering them to the black-eyed, wild animal. The wolf slowly approached Lily and smelled her offering. It grabbed the bones and transformed into a tamed animal.

"Now we will have a wolf with us for the rest of our time in the Overworld," Michael complained.

Simon asked, "What are you going to name it?"

"I think I'm going to call it Wolfie," Lily said with a laugh. The happy wolf stood by his owner's side. Lily was glad that, at long last, something good had come out of their time in the Overworld.

"Is someone going to help me build this igloo?" Michael asked.

An eerie voice replied from the shadows, "I will."

With a start, Lily and Simon turned around to see who had spoken.

8

TRAPPED AND TERRORIZED

"**D**o you need help?" the voice asked again, and let out a sinister laugh.

Lily's tamed wolf stood next to her and barked. The master griefer stepped out of the shadows, smiling, and stood in front of her.

"Are you shocked that I found you?" He laughed again.

"Who are you?" asked Michael.

"You know my name." He let out a louder and more powerful laugh.

"You must be Mr. Anarchy. We know all about your evil tricks," Simon took out his diamond sword and held it tightly.

"We're sorry you're trapped in the Overworld," Lily said to Mr. Anarchy. "We know how it feels. We're also stuck here, and we want to go home. I miss my parents."

"Who said I was trapped here? I can leave any time I want. I love it here. And all I want to do is destroy you."

"Why?" asked Lily.

"When you get back to the village, none of you will have any homes left. I will have blown up your precious little cottage and your wooden home. I've already destroyed Simon's house." His malicious voice boomed throughout the cold biome.

Night was beginning to fall in the Overworld. Michael stared at the half-finished igloo, knowing they weren't going to finish it in time, and they were going to be destroyed by hostile mobs.

Mr. Anarchy looked up at the sky. He pointed his diamond sword at the trio. "You are TPing with me to the jungle."

"We refuse to be your prisoners!" Michael said.

"You have no other choice." He splashed a potion of weakness at them and the group lost hearts.

Michael saw four zombies lumbering toward them. He barely had any hearts left, and he knew he couldn't battle these undead mobs.

"You have no energy. Being with me is better than being destroyed by hostile mobs," Mr. Anarchy said as he clutched a bottle of potion that he threatened to splash on them if they didn't listen to him.

"If we let them destroy us, we'll just respawn in our beds and be away from you!" Lily cried triumphantly.

"Are you sure? What if I've already destroyed your homes, and you don't have beds to respawn in?"

Simon, Lily, and Michael exchanged wide-eyed glances, unsure of what to do. Finally, Simon bowed his head. "I guess we don't have a choice," he said.

Mr. Anarchy forced Lily to make the wolf sit down and stay in the cold biome. Lily was heartbroken. The group reluctantly TPed to the jungle biome and arrived in Mr. Anarchy's jungle temple.

He led them to a small prison cell in the basement. Mr. Anarchy closed the door behind them and laughed, "Good night, my little prisoners."

"We have to find a way to get out of here," said Lily.

"I know," Michael agreed. "This is awful, but we were just going to be destroyed in the cold biome anyway. We had no time to craft that igloo."

The floor was covered in cave spiders. Simon took out his sword and began destroying them. "This place is terrible. I don't want to spend the night in a room filled with spiders."

"There aren't any beds." Lily walked around the small room.

"We have to craft some," said Michael.

As the trio started to craft beds, two skeletons spawned in the prison cell. One shot an arrow at Lily.

"Get them!" She hollered as she rubbed the bruise.

Simon and Michael struck the bony mobs with their swords, but the skeletons were powerful and weren't losing hearts as fast as they hoped. Lily splashed a potion on the skeletons, destroying them.

"We have to finish these beds. Now that Simon's house was destroyed, we have to be able to spawn in one place," Michael said.

"Why would we want to respawn in this horrible prison?" Lily replied.

"But if we don't, where will Simon respawn?" Michael asked.

"Do you think I'll respawn in my own bed at home?" Simon asked hopefully.

"I wouldn't count on it," a voice boomed from the door.

The group looked over and saw Mr. Anarchy standing by the door with a tray of food.

"Dinner is served," he said, and he let out another sinister laugh.

"Why are you feeding us?" asked Lily.

"I want you to get your energy up so I can have some evening entertainment. I love watching you guys try to battle hostile mobs."

"You spawned the skeletons?" asked Michael.

"What do you think?" Mr. Anarchy smiled.

"Are you going to trap us in here and spawn monsters all night?" asked Lily.

Mr. Anarchy shut the door.

Lily whispered to her friends, "Let's get destroyed by the next hostile mob, so we can respawn and get out of here."

Mr. Anarchy opened the door, "I heard you. And I wouldn't do that if I were you. You might be on Hardcore mode."

"What?" Simon screeched.

"I said 'might.'" Mr. Anarchy closed the door.

"That's not fair. You can't do that!" Lily shouted, but it was too late. Mr. Anarchy caused his damage and left them alone to possibly perish on Hardcore mode.

"If we get destroyed on Hardcore mode, we might be wiped from existence." Michael paced around the small room.

"I know! We have to fight hostile mobs and try to figure out a way to escape," said Simon.

Four zombies spawned in their small prison cell. Lily lunged at one of the zombies and used all of her strength to strike the mob. Michael and Simon fought alongside Lily.

"They are losing hearts, but we aren't destroying them," Lily spit out while shielding herself from the zombie.

"I have some potions," Michael pulled a bottle from his inventory and splashed its contents on the zombie, weakening the undead mob.

"Attack!" Michael called to his friends.

The trio annihilated the zombies. They picked up the rotten flesh the zombies dropped and placed it in their inventories.

Lily pulled milk from her inventory and took a sip. She offered it to her friends and whispered, "Where do you think Mr. Anarchy is watching us from?"

She walked along the wall, looking for any holes through which Mr. Anarchy, wearing his blue skin, would be able to peek into the prison and be entertained watching the battle of the trio against whatever hostile mob he spawned next.

"I don't see any holes." Michael put his hand against the wall.

"Me, neither," said Lily.

Simon looked up. "Wait, I think I see something!"

9
IN THE JUNGLE

Simon looked at the floor when he spoke. "He's watching us from the ceiling. I see a light peeking through."

"I think you're right." Lily could see the reflection from the light on the ground.

"We can't climb up there." Michael looked at the cell's dirt floor, not wanting Mr. Anarchy to know they were discussing escaping.

Two skeletons spawned in the corner of the room and Lily sighed, "Not again! This isn't even challenging, just exhausting."

Michael leapt at a skeleton and said, "I have no idea why Mr. Anarchy would want to see us battle skeletons. It's kind of boring. I'd think he'd want to see us fight various hostile mobs."

Lily yelled, "Don't give him any ideas," and then pierced the side of a skeleton with her enchanted diamond sword and destroyed him.

"One down and one to go," Michael remarked, then slayed the final mob.

"I wonder what monster he's going to send us next?" Lily mused. Simon could tell she was hoping it wouldn't be a witch.

The gang didn't have to wait long for another hostile mob invasion. The floor of the prison was flooded with silverfish. Michael hit the pesky insects with his sword.

The others destroyed a creeper that spawned in the center of the room. Lily jumped back when it exploded.

"Creepers aren't cool at all," Lily shouted at the ceiling.

Mr. Anarchy didn't reply. The gang could just imagine him looking through the hole in the ceiling and watching them as if they were his favorite television show. The thought repulsed Lily.

"We have to stop this man. This is awful," Lily cried out.

"Don't worry, Lily," Simon comforted his friend. "I have a plan."

Michael remarked, "It had better be a good one."

Simon whispered, "We need help. Let's use a potion of invisibility and—"

A dozen zombies spawned in front of them. The trio could barely move, and there was no time to discuss their escape; they had to fight for survival.

Lily splashed potions. Michael and Simon struck zombies with their diamond swords.

Three zombies were destroyed, but there were still nine left.

"We can do this," Lily said as she destroyed a fourth monster.

"I hope so," Michael was busy striking the undead beasts with his sword and was tired. This was getting repetitive, and Michael assumed Mr. Anarchy had a larger plan. Michael couldn't believe he found watching them that entertaining.

Lily destroyed two more zombies and called out to Simon, "Help!"

"I'm trying!" Simon knew the battle was futile.

They were losing hope, when the Prismarines ripped open the prison door and helped annihilate the remaining zombies.

Mr. Anarchy wasn't prepared for this plot twist, and he tore into the room, shooting arrows at the Prismarines.

"You won't get away with this," he warned them as he aimed another arrow at Greta. The arrow struck Greta's shoulder and she cried out in pain.

Michael leapt at Mr. Anarchy, his diamond sword puncturing the man's arm. Lily rushed over to the master griefer and splashed a potion of weakness on him just as the Prismarines aimed a sea of arrows at Mr. Anarchy, destroying him.

"We have to get out of here before he respawns." Michael announced, and the gang sprinted from the small prison cell.

They raced through the ornate, spacious jungle temple and onto a path. The road from the temple was thick with leaves, and it was hard to keep track of each other.

Lily looked up at the sky. "It's getting dark."

Michael said, "We should keep going and find a place to build a house."

Simon wanted to escape as quickly as possible. "We don't have time to build a house. We should TP to the village instead."

Everyone agreed, until a familiar face appeared in front of them and shot arrows at the group.

"I'm back!" Mr. Anarchy laughed.

"You're outnumbered," Michael yelled at the master griefer.

"I don't think so," he smiled.

Michael felt an arrow rip through his arm. He turned around to see who shot the arrow, and was shocked to see a group of men dressed in blue. They looked just like Mr. Anarchy, which confused the group. They had no idea which player was Mr. Anarchy.

"I never said I didn't have an army," the master griefer cackled.

Lily was dumbfounded when she saw Mr. Anarchy change his skin in front of them. He went from a blue man to someone dressed in jeans and a red sweater. Lily wondered if Mr. Anarchy had found some setting that allowed him to change skins every few hours.

Mr. Anarchy shot an arrow at Lily. She aimed at the man in the jeans and red sweater, but he disappeared.

When he reappeared, he was wearing black pants and a green shirt. "I can't keep track of him," Lily cried. Although she was glad he didn't look like his soldiers, Lily was confused.

Suddenly, Mr. Anarchy struck Lily with a diamond sword. Her friends were battling his blue-skinned army and weren't able to help her. She had to battle Mr. Anarchy on her own. She leapt toward the master griefer with her enchanted diamond sword, but before she could strike him, he splashed a potion on her, and she lost hearts.

Lily felt her head spin. She grabbed some milk from her inventory and took a sip, as Mr. Anarchy's skin changed to red. She struck the red griefer, but he was too strong, and there was no way Lily would be able to destroy him. This was an impossible battle.

Thunder boomed throughout the Overworld. Lily knew they were about to face another challenge.

10
SURVIVAL IN THE OVERWORLD

Thick, wet drops began to fall on the group. When Mr. Anarchy looked up at the heavy clouds above them, Lily took the opportunity to run toward her friends.

Mr. Anarchy seemed as surprised by the rain as they were, which calmed Lily down, because she knew it was probably just a normal storm, and they wouldn't be attacked by an incredible number of hostile mobs.

"Skeletons!" Michael called out.

Lily looked over. It was just a couple of skeletons, and she let out a sigh of relief. She remembered that, when she'd been new to the game, battling a few skeletons in a rainstorm had been a challenge. But after these few days trapped in the Overworld, she couldn't believe how easy that seemed.

Simon defeated the bony beasts with just a few strikes from his diamond sword and joined the group in their battle against Mr. Anarchy and his army.

Regaining her strength, Lily sprinted toward Mr. Anarchy. He called out, "You're a fearless one, aren't you?"

Lily had to stifle her laughter. It was funny how much she didn't mind fighting other players, but how she'd tense up when she encountered a witch. Yet she replied, "I get pleasure from destroying bullies."

"I'm not a bully," Mr. Anarchy exclaimed.

Lily slammed her sword into the master griefer and he lost hearts. Michael shot an arrow at Mr. Anarchy and he was destroyed.

The trio and the Prismarines annihilated the soldiers. Arrows, swords, and potions flew at the blue soldiers and the skeletons.

When the last blue soldier was destroyed, the sun came out, and Simon announced, "Let's TP to the village."

The group TPed and emerged in the center of town. Juan the Butcher raced over to them. "I'm so glad you're here. There is a strange man who entered the village. He was asking about you guys, and I was worried."

Fred the Farmer stood next to Juan. "He stopped by my house. He wanted to know if I knew a Simon, a Lily, or a Michael."

Michael pondered who the strange man was and asked, "What does he look like?"

Fred described the man, "He's wearing a brown suit."

"I don't know anyone who looks like that," said Michael.

The others agreed. They never met a man in a brown suit.

Lily blurted out, "Oh no! It has to be Mr. Anarchy. He constantly changes his appearance. Is he still here?"

"I'm not sure," said Fred. "He just asked me if you were here and then he left."

Michael wondered when Mr. Anarchy had the chance to enter the town, but it could have been when they escaped from the prison cell with the folks in green jumpsuits.

Lily said, "I know this sounds crazy, but I hope the strange man in the brown suit is Mr. Anarchy, because I wouldn't want another person to be targeting us."

The others agreed. Greta said, "Besides Mr. Anarchy, there aren't too many griefers on this server. I know we used to grief, but I think Mr. Anarchy is the only one who still does."

"Along with his soldiers," added Lily.

Juan reminded them that it was getting dark and they should head inside before hostile mobs of the night began to spawn in the village.

"Too late," Michael said. "I just caught the eye of one of those Endermen."

The friends turned their heads just in time to see two block-carrying Endermen. The one that had spotted Michael let out a loud shriek.

"Run toward the water!" Simon called.

Michael raced toward the lake nearby, but the Enderman was right behind him. He didn't think he'd make it in time. Michael turned around and the Enderman reached for him. He sprinted faster and jumped into the cold, blue water. Both Endermen leapt in after him and were destroyed.

"This is going to be some night," Lily said as she helped Michael climb back out of the water, looking around for any witch huts nearby.

"We need to seek shelter, and I need to dry off," Michael announced to the group. "I have a big house. I think I can offer all of the Prismarines a place to stay."

"What about me?" Simon asked. "I don't have a house."

"You can stay with me," Lily suggested. "I know my cottage is small, but I have enough room."

The gang headed for shelter. They were relieved when they entered the homes without being attacked by hostile mobs.

Lily settled into her bed. She hated being stuck in the Overworld, but she loved the comfort of her bed in the cottage. While she was in bed, she could almost pretend she was just on a beach trip with her family. When she started to think about her family's annual summer vacation, she was both comforted and sad.

"I miss my family," she said to Simon, who was in the bed across from her.

"Me too." Simon's eyes filled with tears.

"I know this is a fun adventure, but I really miss my real life," she confessed.

"I even miss school. I'd do anything to be in Mrs. Sanders's class. I'd take a million hours of lunch detention to get out of this game."

"Remember how excited we were about playing on this server? And how long we spent building that roller coaster?"

Simon nodded his head, "Yes. I think the only way we are going to survive here is if we realize how much we love the Overworld. We might be trapped, but once we begin to enjoy playing the game, I think we might have a better chance of survival. I don't know if that makes any sense."

Lily smiled. "It makes perfect sense."

Simon pulled the covers over his tired body. "I think we should get some sleep. We'll want to respawn here if anything happens to us."

Lily agreed. She said goodnight and they both drifted off to sleep.

They awoke to a beautiful day in the Overworld. The sun was shining. Lily looked out the window and could see cows grazing in the pasture. She heard barking.

"Oh my! It can't be!" She raced to her door and opened it. "It's Wolfie!"

11
WHERE'S MICHAEL?

"I can't believe I was reunited with Wolfie!" Lily was beaming. "I'm so happy!"

Juan rushed over to Lily. "I have bad news. The Prismarines are missing, and so is Michael."

"What?" Lily was shocked.

"I went to deliver some meat to them and nobody was there," Juan said.

Simon and Lily ran to Michael's epic wooden house. They entered the house to search for their friends, but they could tell almost immediately that it was empty.

"Michael," Lily called, her voice echoing in the empty rooms.

"Green people," Simon called out.

"That's not funny. They call themselves the Prismarines," Lily said.

"Okay, but they are green," replied Simon.

"Do you think the Prismarines have anything to do with Michael's disappearance?" Lily asked.

"I don't know, but I'm thinking it has something to do with Mr. Anarchy," Simon said and walked through the house, opening every door and even looking in Michael's fireplace.

Juan walked into the house. "I told you. They are missing. This is horrible."

"We'll find them," Lily said.

"How?" asked Juan.

Lily stammered, "I'm not sure, but I think we should head to the jungle temple to see if this is the work of the evil Mr. Anarchy."

Simon agreed, and the duo set out toward the jungle biome. They grabbed apples from their inventory and plotted their course.

When they finally reached the jungle biome, they heard a whistling in the trees. A moment later, they were hit by a bunch of arrows.

"It's Mr. Anarchy's army," Lily said as she sheltered herself behind a large tree.

Simon aimed his bow and arrow at the griefers, but was only able to strike one. They were skilled fighters.

One of the blue men leapt at Lily and slammed his sword against her body. She was losing hearts.

"You're coming with me," he demanded.

"Simon!" she called out as the soldier herded her away from her friend. Simon turned to run toward Lily.

"You're coming with us, too," another blue griefer demanded.

"But—" The blue man splashed a potion on Simon, and he was weakened and could no longer speak.

"Follow us to the jungle temple," a blue man told them.

Lily and Michael walked toward the temple. The griefers held diamond swords against their backs as they made the journey.

"Look who came back." Mr. Anarchy reappeared, wearing an orange suit.

Lily wanted to ask him if he wore a brown suit earlier, but she didn't have any energy, even to voice a question, and she doubted that he would have answered honestly.

"Did you guys have such a good time, you wanted a return visit?" Mr. Anarchy laughed.

The blue griefer opened the door to the prison cell. Lily looked for Michael and the folks in green jumpsuits, but they weren't there.

"Where are our friends?" she asked weakly.

Mr. Anarchy seemed perplexed. "Why would they be in here?"

"But you—" Lily stopped. She didn't have to explain anything to the master griefer. If he didn't trap her friends, he shouldn't know they were missing.

"What?" Mr. Anarchy knew Lily was withholding information.

"Nothing," Lily replied.

"I think you're hiding something from me." The master griefer grabbed his diamond sword and pointed it at Lily. "Remember, you might be on Hardcore mode."

Lily realized she hadn't been destroyed since Mr. Anarchy had suggested that she and her friends were on Hardcore mode. If she was on Hardcore mode, she feared she could be erased from both the server and her life.

"Michael is missing,"Lily confessed.

"What? Where is he?" The master griefer was annoyed.

"We don't know. We thought he was here," Lily told him.

"No, he's not here, but I am not happy about this. I'm the one who controls the Overworld and I want to know everything," Mr. Anarchy shouted. He ordered his army to find Michael.

Lily was happy to know that someone was going to search for her friend, but she was worried. What if Michael was on Hardcore mode and was attacked and destroyed?

Mr. Anarchy closed the door. Simon and Lily were alone in the prison.

"We have to find Michael before Mr. Anarchy does." Simon paced the length of the small room.

"But how? We're trapped in here." Lily felt defeated.

"I don't know. But I'm also worried because if Mr. Anarchy doesn't have Michael and the Prismarines, then who took them?"

Lily asked, "What if the Prismarines are really bad and they were just pretending to be good?"

"That's a possibility, but I really trusted them," remarked Simon.

"The only way we're going to solve anything is if we can get ourselves out of here." Lily looked at the ground and then exclaimed, "I have the best escape plan!"

"What is it?" asked Simon.

"Do you have any obsidian?"

12
BATTLE OF THE BLAZES

Simon rummaged in his inventory and found some obsidian. He placed it in a rectangle on the ground and ignited a flame. Purple mist surrounded them as they activated the portal.

"What a strange way to escape," Lily said to her friend.

"I know," he agreed. "It's like escaping to the worst place in Minecraft."

"I think we were already in one of the worst places in Minecraft." Lily was happy to leave that small prison cell.

"Agreed," Simon told her as they emerged onto the netherrack landscape and saw a group of blazes and ghasts flying through the sky toward them.

"Do you have any snow left from the cold biome? Or did you give it all to Michael for the igloo that we never completed?" Lily asked her friend.

"I have some left." Simon crafted a snowball and aimed it at the first blaze, destroying the fiery beast.

Lily only had a few snowballs in her inventory and used them sparingly. She only threw them when she knew she would be able to strike and destroy the mob she aimed at.

Simon obliterated another ghast with a snowball. Lily threw a snowball and destroyed the final ghast.

"We should make a portal to the Overworld now and head back to Lisimi Village," suggested Lucy.

"Wait. Look." Simon pointed out a Nether fortress in the distance.

"I don't want to go loot a fortress. I want to find our friends. And the Nether is a lot worse in real life. I knew this was a fiery biome, but it's very hot and seriously creepy. I don't like it here. It's a lot more fun when we are playing the game. I think if I go into the Nether fortress, I won't enjoy it."

Simon disagreed. "Look, this might be our only opportunity to explore a Nether fortress in real life. And we might get some treasure. You know how hard it is to find a Nether fortress."

"I don't care about treasure—I want to find Michael!"

"Lily, we might be stuck here forever," Simon said. "We might need that treasure to survive. This is no joke."

Lily sighed, but she had to admit that Simon had a point. Her inventory was very low and she might not have time to replenish it. Ever since they arrived on this server, she was in a constant battle and had no time to gather supplies.

"Okay," she replied. "Let's go to the Nether fortress. But we have to make it quick."

"Great!" Simon replied, watching his step as he walked. There were many lava streams and he feared they'd fall in one.

"I hope I don't regret this." Lily shook her head.

A group of zombie pigmen walked by them. The duo tried to avoid the mobs. Although they were passive, zombie pigmen could be aggressive if provoked, and Simon and Lily tried hard not to brush against them and make them upset.

Simon suggested they sprint to the Nether fortress.

"Why can't anything be easy?" Lily cried as she looked up and spotted two blazes protecting the Nether fortress. "We should have just hopped in the portal back to the Overworld."

"Don't worry; we can handle these guys." Simon aimed his snowball at the flying menaces. He destroyed one.

"Got it!" Lily destroyed a blaze.

Lily picked up the glowstone dust, as well as a blaze rod from the blaze that Simon destroyed.

"Looks like that's all of them. We can enter the fortress now." Simon walked into the fortress and marveled at its beauty. He had been in countless Nether fortresses while playing the game, but he had never walked into one in real life. He tried to take it all in.

"We should loot this fortress for everything. We are both running low on resources. Everything is valuable," Simon said.

Lily nodded and reached for a patch of Nether wart growing next to soul sand. She was placing the Nether wart in her inventory when she heard a bouncing noise. "I think I hear magma cubes."

"You're right." Simon spotted the blocky mobs jumping in their direction.

Lily slapped her sword against the beasts, cutting the larger magma cube into smaller cubes, which Simon destroyed.

With a cheer, Simon called out, "It's treasure time!"

They walked around the Nether fortress searching for chests.

"I found one!" Lily called out.

There was a hallway with two chests. Simon opened the first.

"Diamonds!" Lily was thrilled. "You were right, Simon. This was a good idea. Now we have all of these valuable gems."

The duo placed the diamonds in their inventory, and Lily opened the second chest. "Enchantment books!" she exclaimed. "These will come in handy."

As they placed the treasures in their inventory, they kept a lookout for any hostile mobs that might be spawning in the dimly lit Nether fortress.

"We should get out of here," suggested Lily.

Simon agreed. As they walked out of the fortress, Lily narrowly avoided being blasted by a ghast's fireball.

Just in time, she made a fist and punched the fireball back toward the ghast to destroy it.

"Nice job!" Simon said. "But look, there are more!" Lily saw a large group of blazes flying toward them.

"Do you think Mr. Anarchy knows where we are, and is punishing us for escaping?" Simon asked as he punched a fireball back at a ghast.

"No, this is just how it is in the Nether," remarked Lily. "That's why I hate it here."

She grabbed her last snowball and threw it at a blaze. The blaze exploded, but another blaze was right behind it. She knew there was no way she'd win this battle on her own. She looked for Simon, but he was no longer fighting beside her.

"Simon! Help!" Lily called out as she aimed her bow and arrow at the blazes.

"Over here," Simon called from atop the portal. "Hop on!"

Purple mist surrounded Simon, and Lily leapt onto the portal, away from the blazes.

13
MOBS AT NIGHT

The portal left them outside of Lisimi Village. It was almost night time, and they hurried toward town.

"We have to get to my cottage before nightfall," Lily urged.

"I thought we'd find Michael today. I feel so discouraged," Simon confessed.

"I know. I thought we'd find him, too." Lily was upset that they'd have to wait even longer to find their friend and the people in green jumpsuits.

"I'm not sure we're going to make it to shelter before the sun goes down." Simon looked at the sky. It was growing dark. A bat flew past him.

"I don't want to spend the night near the swamp." Lily hated the swamp—there was no better place to run into a witch. "And there's a full moon, too!"

"We have no choice." Simon picked out a small patch of grass, "Should we build a small house here? Remember when we built that one in the desert biome?"

Lily just nodded. She didn't want to be reminded of their past adventures, when they had been playing the game from the comfort of their homes.

Two Endermen walked by, and Lily turned her eyes away too late; one of the lanky Endermen shrieked and turned toward her.

"Not again!" Lily was exhausted. She ran toward the murky swamp water, hoping to reach it before the Enderman reached her. Reluctantly, she jumped into the dirty water, luring the Enderman in after her. As she walked back out of the water, she remarked, "At least we have an easy way to destroy Endermen."

"We have to finish this house, fast." Simon chugged milk from his inventory and passed it to Lily.

They finished one wall and placed a torch on it to ward off any hostile mobs. They completed the house in record time, and Lily was relieved when she walked through the front door. She quickly crafted two beds and jumped into one.

"Do you think we'll find Michael?" Lily was worried about her friend and had a hard time falling asleep.

"Yes, but I don't think it's going to be easy."

Lily sighed. "None of this has been easy."

"But you have to admit that finding the diamonds was pretty awesome," Simon said. He thought about all the gems that filled his inventory. He was excited to share them with Michael.

They both drifted off to sleep, but were awoken when an explosion shook their small house.

Kaboom!

"What was that?" Lily asked as she jumped out of bed.

"I don't know." Simon raced to the small window, but he couldn't even see smoke.

"Should we stay in the house? It's dark and it's probably too dangerous to go out. And you know I can't stand the swamp. What if we are attacked by slimes and witches?" Lily paced around the small house.

"We have to find out what happened, and see if anyone needs help." Simon put on his armor.

"Of course. What was I thinking?"

"I know why you're nervous. We're not sure if Mr. Anarchy used command blocks to place us on Hardcore mode."

"Yes, that's true. I don't know what will happen to us if we're destroyed." Lily bit her lip, and her eyes welled with tears.

"The stakes are higher, but we can't let that change who we are. We love to help people."

"You're right," said Lily, nodding and putting her armor on. Then she paused. "Do you hear that?"

There was a muffled sound outside their door. It sounded like someone was talking.

"Do you think someone is trying to blow up our house with TNT?" Lily ran to the door.

Simon followed Lily. When they rushed into the dark swamp, they saw a person standing near the swamp water.

"Lily! Simon!" the person called out to them. "Help!"

It was Michael—and a witch was just about to reach him.

14
STRUGGLE IN THE SWAMP

Lily's fear of witches left her frozen. The witch darted toward Lily, but she stood paralyzed and panicked.

"Michael! Help!" Lily called out.

"I can't!" Michael replied.

Lily looked over and spotted a man in a brown suit standing next to Michael. He was pointing a sword at her friend and Simon was rushing to his side. She knew she must overcome her fear of witches. She had to battle this one alone.

With a deep breath to calm herself, she sprinted toward the witch and swung her diamond sword at the purple-robed witch. She had only fought witches in the game, and now she had to battle the mob in real life. The witch appeared even more sinister and frightening as Lily struck her again with her diamond sword.

The witch splashed a potion on Lily, which weakened her. As she stood in front of the witch, her eyes locked with the evil mob's. Lily wanted to plead for the witch to stop, but she knew it was pointless. Instead, Lily gathered what little strength she had and clobbered the witch. With a final blow from Lily's sword, the witch cried out and then vanished, destroyed.

Lily felt empowered from the battle. She would never be quite so scared to battle a witch again. She felt like she could face any foe in the Overworld without panicking. With a small smile, she ran to help her friends, Michael and Simon.

Simon was aiming his bow and arrow at the man in the brown suit. "You're going down."

"Never!" He said with a laugh.

Lily recognized that laugh and yelled, "You're Mr. Anarchy!"

"No, I'm not!" The man dodged the arrow and leapt toward Simon, clobbering him with his diamond sword. Simon was losing hearts.

Lily sprinted to the man in the brown suit and plunged her diamond sword into his chest.

"You should have worn armor," Lily said as she struck him again, leaving the man incredibly weak. "You know better than that, Mr. Anarchy."

"I'm not Mr. Anarchy," the man said weakly. "Look behind you."

"I don't fall for those sorts of tricks, Mr. Anarchy." Lily held her diamond sword against the man's body.

A voice boomed from behind Lucy. "That's not Mr. Anarchy."

Lily cringed. "What?"

Simon raced to Lily's side and called out, "I'll get him."

"Which one?" Lily was confused. She didn't want to turn around and look at the other Mr. Anarchy. She didn't want to give this man in the brown suit the opportunity to drink a potion that might help him regain his strength, since he only had one heart left.

Lily didn't know if she should deliver the final strike or question him. "Who are you?"

Michael called out. "Guys. There are two Mr. Anarchys. They work together. Destroy this one right now."

Lily struck the man and destroyed him, as the other Mr. Anarchys. screamed, "No!"

"So that's how you're so powerful. You're two people?" Simon questioned as he threatened to splash a potion of weakness on him.

Michael, Lily, and Simon cornered Mr. Anarchy. He replied. "Maybe there are even more of me."

Michael asked, "Where are the Prismarines?"

Mr. Anarchy remained silent.

Michael asked again, "Tell me what you did to the Prismarines. Where are they?"

Mr. Anarchy still didn't say a word.

"Lead us to those people," Michael demanded.

"Maybe he really doesn't know where they are. Maybe the other Mr. Anarchy was in charge," suggested Lucy.

The remaining Mr. Anarchy grabbed a potion from his inventory. The group jumped back to avoid it. They were stunned when he splashed the potion on himself and disappeared.

Once Mr. Anarchy was gone, Simon and Lily turned to Michael. They led him to their small house, where they barely had enough room to craft a bed for their friend.

"What happened to you? We were so worried," said Lily.

Michael explained how the man in the brown suit, who claimed to be Mr. Anarchy, had entered their house with the group of blue soldiers. They'd splashed potions on everyone, depleting everyone's hearts. He had kept them captive in an abandoned mine. The group was exhausted, but they used their pickaxes to break down the wall together and escape from their cell. "We didn't know what to do," Michael told his friends. "Spiders were spawning, and we barely had enough energy to destroy them. But we made our way through the dirty mine, trying to find our way out. Just as we spotted the exit, I overheard the other Mr. Anarchy talking to the blue soldiers. I stopped to spy on their conversation, and when I looked up again, the Prismarines were gone. I didn't know what to do, so I ran as fast and as far as I could. It was getting dark and I was in the swamp biome. That's when I spotted the cottage. But before I could approach the house, Mr. Anarchy appeared and began to threaten me."

"I can't believe there are two Mr. Anarchys. This is going to be a tougher battle than we thought," remarked Simon.

"I know, it's awful," Lily said, and then she suggested they all get some sleep. It would be morning soon, and they needed a place to respawn together if they were destroyed.

"If we respawn at all," Simon reminded her. "What if we are still on Hardcore mode?"

Michael said, "No, there's good news! That's what I heard the other Mr. Anarchy talking about: he said that he was going to use command blocks to put us on Hardcore mode, but he hadn't done it yet. The soldiers said that the other Mr. Anarchy had also threatened it, but didn't do it either. So we're not on Hardcore mode—or, not yet."

Lily let out a sigh of relief. At least they could be destroyed and simply respawn. Although she wanted to get out of the world of Minecraft more than anything, she was happy to know that she wasn't going to be destroyed forever.

The trio fell asleep. When the morning arrived, Lily bounded over to the window. "It's a sunny, nice day. Let's get back to town. I want to get away from the swamp."

The group raced toward the village. As they reached the rows of houses and shops, Juan and Fred approached them. Both of the men spoke fast and at the same time.

"Stop," Simon exclaimed. "We can't understand what you're saying."

Juan spoke first. "The Prismarines. They—"

Fred cut him off. "I think they did something awful."

Michael was shocked. "What?"

"Come, we'll show you." Juan ran toward the roller coaster.

The gang reached the grand coaster and stopped. Half of the ride had been destroyed by TNT.

"Who did this?" Lily cried out.

Fred replied, "Brett and Greta."

15

THE LUCK OF THE DRAW

Lily stared at the rubble in disbelief. All of their hard work had been destroyed. "Isn't it ironic that we got trapped in this game because we were trying to protect this roller coaster, and now it's been destroyed anyway?"

"I can't believe that Brett and Greta did this." Michael shook his head. "I really thought they were our friends."

"We have to rebuild the coaster," Simon announced.

"I think that's the last thing we should worry about now. We have to figure out how to stop both of the master griefers and get back home." Lily couldn't believe how fixated she had once been on building this roller coaster, and how little it meant to her now. However fun that first, thrilling ride had been, that was only a brief enjoyment. She knew now that there were more important matters.

Juan said, "You must find these evil griefers. Not only did the Prismarines destroy your ride, they began to terrorize the town. They splashed potions of harming on innocent townspeople, totally at random."

Fred said, "And they stole crops from my farm. They simply picked a bunch of carrots and placed them in their inventories."

"We have to find the people in green jumpsuits and question them." Michael studied a map as he spoke.

"Where do you think they're hiding? What's on that map?" asked Simon.

"I bet they are working with Mr. Anarchy," Michael said. "I want to head to the jungle temple. There needs to be a showdown."

Lily paused. "Maybe they aren't working with him at all."

"What are you saying?" questioned Michael.

Before Lily could answer, the sky turned dark and a loud roar boomed through the village.

Emily the Fisherwoman raced toward them. "There's a zombie invasion, and someone summoned another Ender Dragon and a Wither."

The Ender Dragon flew toward them with the Wither following closely behind. The powerful dragon let out a roar and banged its scaly wing into the roller coaster, crushing the side of the ride.

"Oh no!" Lily cried out, and she grabbed her bow and arrow from her inventory to aim at the dragon.

Michael dodged Wither Skulls that the Wither shot at them from its three heads. "This is an impossible battle."

Simon reminded him that it could be worse. "At least we're not on Hardcore mode."

Lily thought the Ender Dragon was a lot scarier in real life than it ever had been on her computer screen. The fire-breathing dragon lunged toward her. Simon pelted the beast with a snowball, infuriating the master of the End.

Townspeople rushed to their side to help battle the two mob bosses. Arrows and snowballs flew through the dark, rainy skies.

A horde of zombies and skeletons approached the group, but they couldn't turn their sights from the incredible flying mobs that ruled the Overworld.

Michael aimed another arrow at the Ender Dragon.

Simon shouted, "We have to get the Wither, too."

A townsperson shot an arrow at the Wither. Simon and Lily used up every resource they had in their inventory to destroy the three-headed beast that shot Wither skulls at them.

Lily was in the middle of aiming an arrow at the Wither when she heard familiar voices. Brett, Greta, and the Prismarines were back.

Brett grabbed snowballs from his inventory and threw them at the Wither.

Michael felt his muscles tense with anger at the griefers who had ruined their coaster. With a scowl, he aimed his arrow away from the Wither and shot Brett instead.

Brett was shocked. "Why are you attacking me?"

Simon moved to Michael's side and shot an arrow at Greta.

Greta cried, "What is going on?"

Brett and Greta didn't fight back. They were too stunned that they were being attacked to retaliate.

The other Prismarines didn't notice Brett and Greta being attacked; they were too busy battling the powerful Wither and the Ender Dragon.

As the Ender Dragon flew close to Brett, its muscular wing hit Brett's shoulder and he lost a heart. Greta shot an arrow at the Ender Dragon, while Michael shot another arrow at Greta.

"What are you doing?" Greta yelled, just as Lily used her last arrow to annihilate the Ender Dragon.

Kaboom!

Lily grabbed the dragon egg that it dropped. As she placed it in her inventory, she realized her inventory was completely empty. She had to replenish it, but she didn't know how. Lily looked over at Michael and saw that he and Simon were grappling with Brett and Greta.

"Stop!" Greta pleaded as she dodged Wither skulls. "Can't you see I'm trying to destroy this powerful, three-headed beast?"

"You destroyed our roller coaster," Michael yelled at her.

"No, we didn't," Greta defended herself.

Juan said, "I saw you do it. You blew up half of the roller coaster with TNT and then terrorized the town."

Fred added, "You stole from our town."

"We would never!" said Brett. "We were trapped in an abandoned mine with Michael. While he slept, they forced us to move into another room in the mine's stronghold. In the room, they tortured us with constant attacks from hostile mobs that the man in the brown suit spawned," Brett explained as he skillfully hit the weakened Wither with a snowball, destroying the beast.

A Nether star dropped from the Wither, and Brett made a move to pick it up, but Michael stopped him.

"You don't deserve this!" Michael grabbed the Nether star.

"Michael, I believe Brett," Lily said. "I think Mr. Anarchy's army framed them. They change skins very quickly. I bet the blue soldiers just changed to mimic the Prismarines' appearance."

Michael paused, surprised, when Lily spoke, then nodded as he listened to her theory. "That makes sense. I couldn't imagine these guys attacking us."

"I told you we were innocent," Greta said. "Now, let's find Mr. Anarchy and destroy him."

Lily wasn't sure she should join the others. She had no resources left, leaving her extremely vulnerable. "My inventory is empty," Lily confessed.

Right away, the Prismarines crowded around Lily and handed her arrows, snowballs and potions to refill her inventory. She felt confident they'd be faithful in battle.

16

CALL ME MR. ANARCHY

When the group stormed the jungle temple, they took the blue men completely by surprise. Simon struck two blue griefers with his diamond sword and destroyed them instantly. Mr. Anarchy heard the commotion and sprinted into the thick of the battle.

"This is a pointless fight," he said as he brandished his sword. "I control the Overworld."

"And so do I," a voice boomed.

The group turned around to see another man dressed in the same skin as Mr. Anarchy. Both master griefers wore red suits.

"Which one is the real Mr. Anarchy?" Simon asked.

"You'll never know," one of them said as he splashed harmful potions on the Prismarines.

Lily knew that Mr. Anarchy was a master of disguise. She guessed that there was only one master griefer, but he must have dressed one of his soldiers in the same skin to confuse the group.

Lily looked at the Mr. Anarchy that stood next to her, "I know there aren't two of you. You're too greedy to share control of the Overworld—you want all of that power to yourself."

"You're smart," he said, striking her with his sword and depleting her hearts.

"I don't care if you destroy me. I know I'm not on Hardcore mode."

"How do you know that?" Mr. Anarchy questioned.

"Michael overheard the other Mr. Anarchy saying that you never used command blocks—"

Lily didn't have to finish the sentence. Mr. Anarchy raced toward his twin, his face contorted with rage. He began attacking his double with his diamond sword.

Mr. Anarchy's skin changed into a silver suit, while the other Mr. Anarchy remained the same. Lily was right: there was only one master griefer.

The gang used the chaos that followed as an opportunity to defeat the blue soldiers. As they battled, rain started to fall.

"Stop spawning storms!" Lily shouted at Mr. Anarchy.

Mr. Anarchy was busy annihilating his solider in a red suit, but he replied, "That isn't my storm."

The powerful storm filled the Overworld with lightning and thunder.

Brett, Greta, and the other Prismarines crowded around a blue griefer. They were about to obliterate him when thunder crashed, and a bolt of lightning struck the group. Without warning, the entire group disappeared.

"Brett! Greta!" Michael screamed.

Mr. Anarchy, the man in the red suit, the blue griefers, and the trio all stopped and stared.

"Where did they go?" Lily asked.

Mr. Anarchy said, "I think they went home."

"Home?" Lily cried. "How?"

"The lightning." He looked at the sky.

"Have it strike me!" Lily demanded.

"I don't have control over this storm," he confessed.

"I thought you controlled the Overworld," Michael said, leaping at Mr. Anarchy with his diamond sword.

Mr. Anarchy didn't reply. He simply struck Michael with his sword and destroyed him.

"You're all going to be destroyed!" Mr. Anarchy shouted. "You'll never make it home."

Lily ran up behind Mr. Anarchy, splashing a potion of weakness on him. She called out to the others, "Let's end this fight and get out of here."

Simon grabbed bedrock from his inventory and crafted a small house quickly. "This is your new home, Mr. Anarchy."

Mr. Anarchy hollered, "You can never trap me in there."

"We'll see about that," Michael called out.

The trio cornered Mr. Anarchy and herded him into the bedrock prison, but before they could close the structure, he splashed a potion of invisibility on himself and disappeared.

"I hope that's the last time we see him," Lily said, but she knew that was doubtful.

"We can't worry about him," Michael said, "I think we scared him a lot. We also saw that he isn't as powerful as he claims."

They all hurried out of the jungle biome toward the town. The blue griefers didn't follow them. None of them could stop thinking about the folks in green jumpsuits getting back to the real world. Each player secretly envied them.

Lily said, "I'm happy for Brett and Greta. It gives me hope that we can return."

"Are we sure they actually made it back to the real world?" asked Michael. "Maybe they were destroyed forever."

Lily shuddered. She didn't want to imagine such an awful thing. "I think Mr. Anarchy's reaction was very telling. He has seen this before."

"I agree with you. I think he's definitely seen this before. I just wish he wasn't so evil. I wish he'd work with us. He's very smart, and if we worked together, I bet we'd find a way to get out of this game," said Michael.

The group trekked back to the town. They were exhausted from their battle with Mr. Anarchy. They walked to Juan's butcher shop to get some meat and cook a big feast.

"We have to make the best of being trapped in the Overworld," Michael said as he filled his inventory with a bunch of meat for dinner.

"I know," Lily said, "but we also have to find a way to get out of here."

"Remember, Brett and Greta were here a long time," said Michael.

Simon added, "And so were the other Prismarines."

Michael said, hopefully, "We'll get out of here, too."

"Before we go, we have to rebuild the roller coaster and ride it again. Riding the coaster in real life was totally awesome," said Simon.

The gang was excited to get back to their homes. Simon had many ideas for rebuilding his home.

17
SAFE AND SOUND

Weeks passed with no sign of Mr. Anarchy. The gang rebuilt Simon's home, Lily was reunited with Wolfie, and every day the friends kept an eye out for the master griefer.

One day, Juan the Butcher showed up and asked if they wanted to throw a party with the townspeople.

Lily still didn't feel like going to a party. She refused to accept that they might never leave the game, and she missed her family. Still, Simon convinced her that it would be a good idea.

At the party, Lily spoke to a player named Warren. He was also trapped in the Overworld. "Is everyone on this server trapped like we are?" she asked.

Warren replied, "Yes."

Lily wondered how that had happened. Was it simply bad luck that they had all picked the wrong server?

"Aren't you sad being trapped on here?" she asked Warren.

"Yes, we are all strategizing ways to get home," he explained.

"Us, too. I thought that once our friends, the Prismarines, escaped, they'd find a way to get us out of here."

Lily kept hoping Brett and Greta would return and help them escape, but she never heard from them again. The more time passed, the more certain she felt that the Prismarines had left their server to avoid the glitch that could zap them back into the game. She couldn't blame them. Once she and her friends escaped, she'd start a life on a new server and create a new bungalow and roller coaster. She wouldn't risk being trapped here again.

She was happy to talk to Warren. Lily wanted to make new friends. She hoped it would fill the void that Brett and Greta's disappearance had left. She looked at Warren. "Do you like roller coasters?'

"Yes," he replied.

"My friends and I built an awesome one. It was destroyed, but we just rebuilt it. Want to go on a ride?" asked Lily.

"Everyone in town has admired that coaster. They'd all love to go on a ride, but we weren't sure if you wanted other people to use it."

"Yes, anyone can ride it," Lily said, calling Michael and Simon over. "Do you realize that we spent such a long time building that roller coaster and we never invited anyone to ride on it? I feel like we're as bad as Mr. Anarchy and are just looking out for ourselves."

Michael reflected on what Lily said, "We should invite the entire town to ride our coaster. They'd love it."

Simon agreed and then announced, "Everyone in town, listen up! If you want to ride on the roller coaster we constructed, come with us. We will let you ride it."

The townspeople gathered around Simon and everyone walked toward the ride. Simon looked at all the villagers' thrilled faces.

"Wow," remarked Lily, "I can't believe we've been riding this coaster all the time and never offered anyone a ride. I bet everyone must have disliked us."

Warren smiled. "I think they just thought you guys stuck together."

"No." Lily felt awful that this was the way the other players had perceived them. "We want to be friends with everyone in town. It's just been a whirlwind since we arrived. We were captured. We were trying to adjust to life. We met the Prismarines and didn't know if they were actually our friends." Lily rattled off a million excuses and finally just said, "I'm sorry. I realize we must have seemed very cliquish."

Warren nodded his head.

"I hope you'll give us a second chance?"

As she looked at everyone gathered in front of the coaster, she realized that if they worked together with the other players who were stuck in the game, they'd have even more help when plotting their escape from the Overworld.

"After we all ride the coaster," Lily announced to the group lined up to ride the coaster, "we should have a meeting about trying to get back to the real world."

Everyone cheered. Lily was glad they were going to work together to get out of the server. She climbed into a minecart and as the coaster made its first big dip, Lily giggled, and realized it was the first time she had felt happy in very long time.

18
NEW FRIENDS

Juan the Butcher offered the group various meats and the gang indulged in a large, festive meal.

Simon and Lily were savoring their chicken when Michael walked over and said, "It's been a crazy few days in this new world."

Simon remarked, "It has been. I'm glad that we met new friends, and I'm also happy that Greta and Brett were able to go back home. I'll miss them."

Warren joined the group. Lily said, "We were just talking about how nice it is to meet people like you."

Warren blushed. "There are a lot of other people in town. I can't wait to introduce you to them."

"We want to meet them. It seems, despite being trapped and adjusting to life on this server, we are lucky to be surrounded by new friends," Michael added.

"I'm sorry we were so self-absorbed when we got into this server." Lily was still feeling sorry for not

97

noticing that the townspeople wanted to ride the coaster. They had been too caught up in their battle with Mr. Anarchy and working with the Prismarines to notice anyone else. Lily promised herself that she would use her newfound courage to always watch out for other people.

Simon reminded them they were going to have a meeting where the town could work together and find a way off the server.

Warren exclaimed, "I'd be happy to lead the meeting."

"That sounds like a plan," Simon smiled.

Warren said, "I have a bunch of cake in my inventory. I think we deserve some dessert before we start planning our ways to get off the server."

Lily, Simon and Michael ate the cake and thanked Warren. When they were finished, Warren stood in the center of the town and announced, "Everyone. We are going to have a town meeting. We're going to discuss ways to get back to the real world."

The group cheered. Simon, Lily, and Michael looked out at the crowd of smiling faces. They knew that with this group of new friends, anything was possible.

Check out the rest of the
Unofficial Minetrapped Adventure series
and read what happens to Simon, Lily, and Michael:

Trapped in the
Overworld

WINTER MORGAN

Mobs in the
Mine

WINTER MORGAN

Terror on a
Treasure Hunt

WINTER MORGAN

Ghastly Battle

WINTER MORGAN

Creeper Invasion

WINTER MORGAN

Attack of the
Ender Dragon

WINTER MORGAN

Available wherever books are sold!

DO YOU LIKE FICTION FOR MINECRAFTERS?

Check out other unofficial Minecrafter adventures from Sky Pony Press!

Invasion of the Overworld
MARK CHEVERTON

Battle for the Nether
MARK CHEVERTON

Confronting the Dragon
MARK CHEVERTON

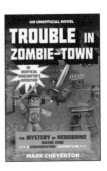
Trouble in Zombie-town
MARK CHEVERTON

The Quest for the Diamond Sword
WINTER MORGAN

The Mystery of the Griefer's Mark
WINTER MORGAN

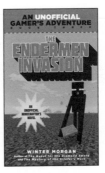
The Endermen Invasion
WINTER MORGAN

Treasure Hunters in Trouble
WINTER MORGAN

LIKE OUR BOOKS
FOR MINECRAFTERS?

Then check out other novels
by Sky Pony Press.

Pack of Dorks

BETH VRABEL

Boys Camp: Zack's Story

CAMERON DOKEY,
CRAIG ORBACK

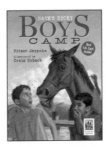

Boys Camp: Nate's Story

KITSON JAZYNKA,
CRAIG ORBACK

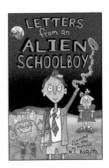

Letters from an Alien Schoolboy

R. L. ASQUITH

Just a Drop of Water

KERRY O'MALLEY CERRA

Future Flash

KITA HELMETAG MURDOCK

Sky Run

ALEX SHEARER

Mr. Big

CAROL AND MATT DEMBICKI